THE AMAZING DRAGONFLIES

G T Evans

This Book belongs to The Amazing

Your Name: _____

"Their fearless flying is known by all,
So gather round and hear my call.

Crowds go wild when they take to the skies,
Come and see with your very own eyes!"

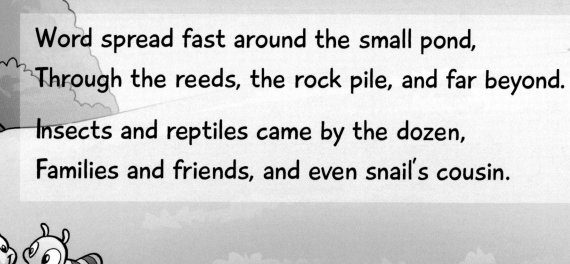

Word spread fast around the small pond,
Through the reeds, the rock pile, and far beyond.

Insects and reptiles came by the dozen,
Families and friends, and even snail's cousin.

But why had they come here? I'm sure you'd like to know,
Why to see The Amazing Dragonflies put on a show.

When all the pond creatures had taken a chair,
And a feeling of excitement had filled the air.

Suddenly as if from nowhere, three dragonflies took flight,
They soared through the air, what an incredible sight.

They looped and twirled and flew close to the water,
They zoomed by the crowd and winked at frog's daughter.

The crowd drew breath as the dragonflies gained height,
Their drop into a barrel roll gave everyone a fright.

"Dragonflies you're the greatest" the pond creatures yelled,
It was touch and go, but the synchronised spin held.

But watching the show from his nest up a tree,
Was a nasty old crow deciding what to have for his tea.

He knew the flying insects would be delicious to eat,
He could find an easier meal but fancied a special treat.

He left his nest with one thought on his mind,
The idea was to stay low and attack from behind.

He weaved through the undergrowth biding his time,
Then appeared on their tails as they began another climb.

The poor dragonflies were completely unaware,
But the crowd saw the crow and shouted "BEWARE!".

As the crow got close and was about to bite,
The dragonflies spotted him and banked to the right.

Diving into the woods hoping to lose him in the trees,
They swerved in and out, but he followed them with ease.

Whooshing through the treetops, back into the sky,
The crowd was getting scared now, as the dragonflies flew by.

Faster and faster the hungry crow gained speed,
Finally, he struck, it was a major blow indeed.

Down and down the injured dragonfly fell,
Would the crow catch him? Nobody could tell.

He opened his beak to scoop up his meal,
But felt a sharp pain and let out a Squeal.

He may not have plunged into the pond if he'd known,
That dragonflies have a nasty bite of their own!

The soaking wet bird looked tired and beat,
As the injured Dragonfly got to his feet.

His wing still hurt thanks to that nasty old crow.
But the Dragonflies were determined to finish the show.

The team took flight, happy to be alive,
The big finale involved a fast-spinning dive.

The manoeuvre was flawless it had been a magnificent day,
The crowd called for more, but the dragonflies couldn't stay.

As they left the small pond the creatures clapped and cheered,
And as quietly as a mouse the crow disappeared.

Back to his nest in the tree he did go.
With a hungry belly, and a bruised ego.

THE END

Made in United States
Orlando, FL
03 June 2022

18464956R00020